The Light Between Us

Brookleigh Bay, Volume 4

Dorothy Blakemore

Published by Mustard Seed Press, 2026.

This is a work of fiction. Similarities to real people, places, or events are entirely coincidental.

THE LIGHT BETWEEN US

First edition. May 4, 2026.

ISBN: 978-1067634971

Written by Dorothy Blakemore.

The Light Between Us

Brookleigh Bay Book 4

Dorothy Blakemore

Psalm 18:28 ESV
For it is you who light my lamp;
the LORD my God lightens my darkness.

Chapter 1

The light over Brookleigh Bay was never still. That was the first thing Marie had learned as a girl, with a paintbrush in her hand — the North Sea was a thief, always stealing colours from the sky and turning them into something colder, deeper, impossible to pin down.

This morning it was a pale, watery gold, slipping through the kitchen window and pooling across the table. Steam curled from the kettle, softening the edges of everything. Marie watched the light catch the rim of Josh's cereal bowl and found herself mixing the colours in her head.

Titanium white.

A wash of yellow ochre.

Payne's grey gathering in the corners.

"Mum! I can't find my gym bag!" Josh's voice carried down the stairs, followed by the heavy thud of feet taking them two at a time.

Marie did not flinch. When the kettle clicked off, she fetched the mugs from the cupboard, her movements automatic.

"It's behind the umbrella stand," she called. "Where you left it yesterday."

A pause. Shuffling. Then, grudgingly, "Oh. Yeah."

She allowed herself the smallest smile.

Luke appeared in the doorway a moment later, Joseph warm and heavy against his shoulder. The baby's fist was curled into the fabric of Luke's T-shirt, his cheek pressed sleepily against his father's collarbone. Luke looked tired — the kind of tired that lived under the skin — but he smiled when he saw her.

"Morning, love." He leaned in to kiss her cheek, smelling faintly of peppermint and his shower gel. "You all right?"

"Yes. You?" she asked, smoothing a crease from his shoulder. A small act of maintenance.

She was good at maintenance.

"Getting there." He shifted Joseph gently. "The lads are already on site — the new-build's behind again because of all this rain. And I've got to stop by the school later. They want a quote for an extension, so I might as well go when I drop Josh off."

He passed the baby over to her.

"I changed Joseph, by the way — but you have what he really wants."

"I noticed the lack of emergency," she said softly. "And yes, I'll feed him when you all go. Then we can sit down in peace for a while."

Luke huffed a quiet laugh.

A sudden crash sounded from the living room. Then delighted giggling.

Marie closed her eyes briefly. "Caleb."

Right on cue, their nearly two-year-old appeared in the doorway, curls wild, dragging a wooden tray behind him like captured treasure.

Luke looked down. "That was on the bookshelf."

Caleb grinned, triumphant.

Josh thundered into the kitchen, hair sticking up at the back, gym bag slung over one shoulder. "Dad, are you still taking me? We've got football practice before assembly."

"Yes, come on then." Luke reached for his coffee. "Grab your coat."

Josh hesitated for half a second, eyes flicking between his parents in a way that felt older than six. "You'll be there for Friday, right? For the play?"

Marie felt something tighten in her chest.

"I said I would, didn't I?" Luke replied, steady and sure. "Front row if I can."

Josh nodded once, satisfied, and disappeared into the hall.

Luke squeezed Marie's hand as he passed her. A brief, grounding pressure.

"I'll get him to school on time."

"I know you will," she said.

The door banged behind them, and the house exhaled into a different kind of noise. Joseph began kicking in her arms, hungry now. Caleb toddled in circles around the table, chanting something unintelligible and joyful.

Marie settled into an armchair to feed Joseph and then placed him into the bouncer near the radiator. His feet kicked enthusiastically at the hanging fabric shapes, laughter bubbling up in bright bursts. She wiped cereal from the table. Retrieved an ornament from Caleb. Redirected him from climbing onto a cupboard. Her body moved constantly.

Her mind drifted elsewhere.

Upstairs. To the wardrobe. Top shelf, back corner. The acceptance letter was still there. *We are delighted to offer you a place on the Fine Art programme at the School of Art.* She had unfolded it so often the centre crease had split clean through. She had kept it anyway.

Proof that once, someone had looked at her work and said yes.

Behind it sat a sketchbook, its elastic had gone slack with time. Then there was a canvas that held a half-finished study of the bay at dusk — bruise-coloured sky, restless water, a horizon that refused to settle. She had meant to go back to it. The sea was there. The sky was there. But the light over Brookleigh Bay — the part that made the whole thing alive — was still missing.

Then had come the positive test, marriage, sickness. Then Josh. Then life, moving forward in practical, necessary steps. She had traded the infinite horizon of a canvas for these four sturdy walls.

Caleb tugged at her jeans, demanding to be lifted. She picked him up automatically, breathing in the warm, milky scent of him. Joseph squealed from the bouncer. The room was scattered with toys.

She loved this. She loved Luke fiercely, with a devotion that sometimes frightened her. He had never asked her to give anything up. Not once. He had even bought her sketchpads and tried to encourage her. Told her more than once that she should make time for it.

But in the shifting grey-gold light of the kitchen, a cold thought pressed in, *had she trapped him*? Luke never complained. She wondered if he ever stood at a window frame on one of his sites and imagined driving past it — past the estate, past the bay — just to see what else there might have been?

Or was she the only one who still felt the ghost of a different life brushing at her shoulder?

Joseph's delighted shriek shattered the thought. Caleb wriggled down from her arms and immediately began attempting to climb the cupboard door.

Marie turned the tap on full, the rush of water loud and steady, drowning out the distant sigh of the sea. There was breakfast to clear. Nappies to change. A day to get on with.

And the light over Brookleigh Bay shifted again, impossible to hold.

Chapter 2

Luke woke before the alarm. February light pressed thin and grey against the curtains, the house suspended in that fragile quiet before morning properly began. For a moment he lay still, listening. The hum of the boiler. Wind rattling faintly along the guttering. Marie's breathing beside him.

It was her he always listened for first. Her breath was steady, but there was tension in it — a faint catch at the end of each exhale, as if even in sleep she were holding something back.

He turned his head slightly. A strand of hair lay across her cheek. Shadows lingered beneath her eyes that had not been there a year ago. Two under two would do that to anyone, he supposed. Three children in six years. School runs and teething and night feeds layered on top of one another like bricks laid without time for mortar to set. But this felt like more than tiredness.

Marie had always moved through their days with quiet competence. She remembered everything — Josh's reading diary, Caleb's favourite cup, the exact strength he preferred his tea after a late finish. She noticed when he was carrying stress before he said a word.

Lately, though, she had been smiling too quickly. Saying "I'm fine" before he had even asked. As if she were tidying something invisible away before he could see it. He brushed his thumb gently across her hand where it rested on the duvet. She shifted but didn't wake.

He wished she would tell him what was wrong. He also knew she probably did not think anything was wrong. That was Marie's way — carry it quietly, do not add to the weight. She had stopped painting at the kitchen table months ago. The sketchpads he bought her still sat where she left them.

He slipped from the bed carefully and dressed in the half-light.

By nine o'clock, he was standing in the staffroom at Brookleigh Bay Primary, the smell of instant coffee and poster paint wrapping around him with nostalgic familiarity. He had called in the day before, but neither the headmaster nor Mrs Hargreaves had been free to see him. Now Daniel Harper stood by the table, one hand braced against the back of a chair, while Mrs Hargreaves sat beside him, glasses low on her nose, spreading rough sketches across the table.

"We've had more admissions than expected," Daniel said. "And if projections hold, we'll be stretched even further next year. We need an extension as soon as possible. How quickly do you think it can be done?"

He studied the drawings. He could see it already: a solid extension off the main

building, practical and in keeping with the rest of the school. He traced a line along one of the rough plans as he spoke, explaining how they could cordon off the site safely during term time and join the buildings properly over the summer holidays.

"We can make it work," he said. "I'll have proper plans to you next week. We could get it ready for the September intake."

Building things — measurable, solid things — was the one place doubt rarely found him. His company was in demand for a reason: they delivered what they promised, and the quality was always worth the cost.

Mrs Hargreaves asked for projected costs and timelines for the governors, while Daniel wanted to know how soon groundwork could begin if approval came through.

"I can't give you the minute details until the plans are finalised," Luke said, glancing between them. "But next week is doable."

The architect would push back, he knew. But it could be done. He assured them he would return with the plans, and if they were approved, work could begin the following week.

On his way back to the office of Linton Builders, his mind drifted to their first flat above the chip shop on Harbour Road. The constant hiss of the fryer downstairs. The smell of hot oil clinging to curtains, to clothes, to canvases propped against the wall.

Marie had painted in the tiny front room because there was not enough space anywhere else. Cross-legged on the floor in one of his old university jumpers, hair twisted up with a paintbrush shoved through it. The window would fog with grease-heavy air, and she would wipe a clear circle with her sleeve so she could see the street below. She worked with a focus that bordered on reverence. He used to stand in the doorway and watch her hands move. Confident. Certain.

One night the boiler flared so loudly it made her jump, and she dragged a streak of ultramarine straight across her cheek without noticing. He had crossed the room and wiped it away with his thumb. She had grinned at him as if he were the only person in the world. He could not remember the last time he had seen her that absorbed in something.

The memory faded as the office came into view. He dropped the folder on Caroline's desk for her to handle the paperwork, explained what the plan was and asked her to get in touch with the architect, then picked up the clipboard for his next job.

The new-build estate was already in motion when he arrived. Vans lined the gravel road, radios murmured from open cab doors, and the rhythmic thud of hammers carried across the site. George had the men organised, as always — foundations checked, safety barriers in place, everyone where they needed to be. The banner for the Considerate Construction Scheme that his dad had enrolled them in before he passed a few years ago was evident at the site entrance.

Luke walked the length of the road, clipboard tucked beneath his arm, hard hat on his head. He paused inside Plot 14. This one was still waiting for its turn — the crew were working on the far side of the estate today, leaving the skeletal frame quiet for the moment. He stepped through the empty doorway and looked out through the open window frame. From here, you could just see a sliver of the bay. Steel-coloured today. Restless.

He checked the delivery schedule. 14 February. He frowned — not at the Valentine's reminder scribbled in the corner — but at the month printed beneath it in the project timeline. August. Their anniversary. Seven years.

Seven years since they had married. Marie's hands had trembled in his as they had said vows the weight of which neither of them had fully understood. Back then, she had talked about exhibitions. About applying for residencies. About painting the coastline in every season until she understood it completely. He had believed she would.

He leaned his shoulder against the bare stud wall and exhaled slowly. When had he last done something that told her she was seen? Not as Mum. Not as the axis their home turned on. But as Marie. He pulled out his phone and ordered a large mixed bouquet from the flower shop.

Work had grown each year thanks to his dad's hard work. Housing projects. Contracts. Payroll. The constant pressure of keeping other families secure. And Marie never complained. Never asked for space. Never said she missed anything. Maybe that was the problem. Maybe she had stopped asking because she thought there was nothing to gain.

He closed his eyes briefly, the wind moving through the open frame. "Lord," he said quietly, voice rough in the hollow shell of the house, "show me how to love her better. I don't know what she needs. But You do."

The prayer was not polished. It did not need to be. It steadied him. When he opened his eyes, the skeleton of the room around him felt less like unfinished work and more like possibility. A structure waiting to be shaped.

He did not know exactly what he would do. Marie was not one for grand gestures or public displays. She would probably hate that. But he would find something that spoke her language. Something patient. Something thoughtful. Something that told her he saw the parts of her she tucked away on high shelves. He could not fix what he did not understand. But he could start by paying attention. And for the first time in weeks, that felt like a foundation he could build on.

Chapter 3

By late afternoon on Friday, the house was warm with the familiar sounds of home — the tumble dryer humming, the boys thundering up and down the hallway, the faint clatter of pans from the kitchen. Luke had showered after work, the steam loosening the cold from his bones, and now he sat cross-legged on the living-room rug with Caleb on one knee and Josh sprawled beside him.

"Watch this," Luke said, lining up three toy cars in a neat row. "You've got to flick them just right. Not too hard, not too soft."

Josh narrowed his eyes with exaggerated seriousness. "Like Goldilocks?"

"Exactly like Goldilocks," Luke said, flicking the first car. It shot across the rug, bounced off the sofa, and spun dramatically onto its side.

Caleb squealed, clapping his hands. "Go! Go! Go!"

Josh flicked his own car, tongue poking out in concentration. His shot was cleaner, straighter, landing perfectly between two cushions.

"Yes!" Josh punched the air. "Beat you!"

Luke held up both hands in surrender. "All right, champ. Best of three."

Caleb attempted his turn, mostly succeeding in throwing the car straight up and nearly hitting Luke in the chin. Luke caught it mid-air and laughed.

"Nice try, little man."

Caleb beamed as if he had won the whole game.

From the kitchen, Marie listened to their laughter as she stirred the sauce on the hob. The sound warmed something in her chest. She glanced over her shoulder into the living room. Luke was leaning back on one hand, Caleb climbing over him like a determined little mountain goat, Josh explaining the rules of a game Luke had invented only thirty seconds ago. They looked... happy.

She swallowed, turning back to the chopping board. The flowers Luke had sent earlier sat in a jug by the window — bright, generous, unexpected. She had not known what to say when they arrived. She still did not. Gratitude and guilt had tangled together in her chest in a way she could not quite name.

"Dinner's ready!" she called.

The boys barrelled into the kitchen, Caleb chanting "pasta! pasta!" as if it were the only word he knew. Luke followed, scooping Caleb up before he could climb onto the table.

They ate together, the way they always did — Josh talking about football practice, Caleb dropping more food than he managed to eat, Joseph babbling happily in his highchair. Luke kept the conversation going, asking Josh about the play, making Caleb giggle by pretending his fork was a tiny aeroplane.

Marie watched them, her fork paused halfway to her mouth. She loved this, but the tiredness pressed at her temples like a thumbprint.

After the plates were cleared, Luke nodded toward the living room. "Family Bible time."

Josh ran to fetch the family Bible from the shelf. Caleb toddled after him, clutching a half-eaten breadstick. They gathered on the sofa, Joseph on Marie's lap, Caleb wedged between his parents, Josh leaning against Luke's shoulder.

Luke opened to the bookmarked page. "Right. Tonight we're in Matthew."

Josh straightened, ready to listen. Caleb immediately tried to turn the pages himself. Luke gently moved his hand aside.

He read the passage slowly, his voice steady and warm. Marie listened, letting the familiar words wash over her. *Come to me, all you who are weary and burdened...*

Her throat tightened.

When Luke finished, he closed the Bible and looked at the boys. "So what does that mean?"

Josh answered first, earnest as ever. "It means Jesus helps when we're tired."

"Exactly," Luke said. "He doesn't expect us to do everything on our own."

Marie stared at her hands.

Caleb offered his own interpretation by shouting, "Jesus!" and throwing his breadstick in celebration.

Luke laughed. "Close enough."

They prayed together — simple, unpolished words — and then Josh leapt up. "Chocolate time!"

Caleb squealed, already running toward the cupboard where the treat box someone had given the family was kept. Luke retrieved it, holding it high until both boys were bouncing on their toes.

"One each," he said. "Choose wisely."

Josh picked a caramel swirl. Caleb grabbed the first thing his hand touched. Marie took a small, dark chocolate, more out of habit than desire. Luke chose last, as he always did.

When the excitement settled, Luke checked his watch. "Right, team. Let's get ready. We need to be at the school by half six."

Josh shot up the stairs to find his costume. Caleb followed, shouting "play! play!" as if he were the star of the show.

Marie stood, smoothing Joseph's hair. "I'll get his bag ready."

Luke touched her arm lightly. "I'll help."

She nodded, though she was not sure what she needed help with. The flowers caught her eye again — bright against the fading light. For a moment, the house felt full of possibility. Not perfect. But held together somehow. And as they gathered coats and shoes and school bags, the evening stretched ahead — ordinary, familiar, and somehow hopeful.

Chapter 4

The school hall smelled of floor polish and poster paint, the kind of scent that clung to every primary school in the country. Rows of plastic chairs stretched out in neat lines, already half-filled with parents shrugging off coats and waving at familiar faces. Fairy lights looped across the stage curtain, twinkling unevenly as if they were trying their best.

Luke held the door open as Josh darted inside, clutching his costume bag to his chest. Caleb toddled after him, determined to keep up, while Marie adjusted the soft sling across her shoulder, Joseph warm and heavy against her chest.

"Straight to your classroom, Josh," Luke reminded him. "Mrs Peters said she wants everyone ready early."

Josh nodded, already half-lost in the crowd of excited children. "See you after! Love you, Mum! Love you, Dad!"

Marie felt the words land warm and soft. Luke smiled, lifting a hand in return. "Love you too, pal."

They found seats halfway down the hall, close enough for Josh to see them but not so close that Marie felt exposed. Ben and Julie were in the row in front and turned around to chat.

Julie beamed. "There you are! Robbie's been buzzing since lunchtime. He says he and Josh have a "very important scene' together."

Ben chuckled, slipping his arm around his wife. "He's been practising his lines in the bath. Nearly drowned the rubber duck giving it stage directions."

Marie smiled, the image tugging something lighter inside her. "Josh has been the same. He kept doing his "brave knight voice' while brushing his teeth."

“Oh, Robbie loves that,” Julie said. “He says Josh is the best at remembering what everyone else is supposed to say.”

“That sounds like him,” Luke said, shifting Caleb onto his lap. “He’s been reciting the whole script at home. Even the bits that aren’t his.”

Ben laughed. “Robbie told us Josh helped him learn the last page. Said he wouldn’t let him give up.”

Marie’s chest tightened — pride, and something softer. “They’re good for each other.”

“They really are,” Julie agreed. “Robbie’s been so much more confident this term. Josh has been a big part of that.”

Marie blinked, caught off guard by the warmth of it. “That’s... lovely to hear.”

Julie reached back to squeeze her hand. “You’re doing a great job, you know.”

Marie opened her mouth, but the words tangled. She managed a small nod.

Joseph stirred in the sling, his tiny fingers curling against her blouse. She rocked gently on instinct, the motion soothing him back into sleep. Caleb bounced on Luke’s knee, full of restless energy. The noise in the hall swelled — laughter, chatter, the scrape of chairs. Marie felt it all pressing in, a soft but insistent weight.

Luke leaned closer. “You all right?”

She nodded. “Just... busy in here.”

He didn’t push. Instead, he shifted Caleb slightly and rested his free hand on hers, warm and steady.

The lights dimmed. A hush rippled across the hall. Mrs Peters stepped onto the stage, smiling with the kind of calm only a seasoned teacher possessed.

“Thank you all for coming,” she said. “The children have worked very hard on tonight’s performance, and we hope you enjoy it.”

The curtain opened.

Josh stood in the second row, next to his best friend, Robbie, wearing a cardboard shield and a slightly crooked paper crown. When he spotted them, his face lit up — a bright, unguarded grin that made Marie's breath catch. He still needed them. Both of them. Even if she felt like she was fading around the edges, he still looked for them.

The play unfolded in a whirl of enthusiastic lines, missed cues, and the kind of earnest acting only children could manage. Josh delivered his lines with surprising confidence, projecting his voice just as Mrs Peters had taught them. Caleb clapped wildly every time Josh spoke, regardless of whether it was appropriate.

Luke laughed quietly, pressing a kiss to the top of Caleb's head. "That's your brother," he whispered.

Marie watched Josh, her chest tightening with something sharp and tender all at once. Pride. Love. And beneath it, a flicker of grief for the version of herself who had once believed she could fill the world with colour.

When the final song began, Josh scanned the audience again until he found them. His smile widened. He waved — small, quick, but unmistakably for them both. Marie lifted her hand in return, blinking hard.

The applause at the end was thunderous. Parents surged forward with cameras and hugs. Luke lifted Caleb onto his hip and nodded toward the classroom door. "Go on. He'll want to see us."

Marie hesitated. "Together?"

"Of course."

They threaded through the crowd. Joseph stirred again, and Marie cupped his head gently as she walked. Josh burst out of the classroom just as they reached the doorway.

"Mum! Dad! Did you see? I didn't forget any of my lines!"

Marie pulled him into a hug. "You were brilliant. Absolutely brilliant."

Luke ruffled his hair. "You were fantastic, Josh. Really fantastic."

Josh hugged them both at once, arms stretched wide, crown slipping sideways. "I saw you. I looked and you were both there."

Marie's throat closed. Luke's hand found her back, steadying.

"Always," Luke said quietly. "We'll always be there."

They walked back to the car together, the cold evening air sharp against their cheeks. The boys chattered the whole way, their excitement spilling over in tangled sentences.

Marie settled Joseph into his seat, her hands steady even as her thoughts swirled. The flowers at home. Luke's gentleness. Josh's smile when he saw them both.

Something inside her shifted — not enough to lift the heaviness, not yet, but enough to let in a thread of light.

Luke closed the car door and glanced at her. "Ready?"

She nodded. "Yes."

And for the first time in a long while, she almost meant it

Chapter 5

Marie had taken the little ones to her mother-in-law's house and had a cup of tea with her. After that she had not meant to go anywhere. The days had simply stretched too wide. Joseph fed, slept, and fed again, his small body ruled by uncomplicated cycles. Caleb, twenty-three months old and newly confident on unsteady legs, had entered a phase of quiet, methodical destruction. He stacked blocks with grave concentration, only to roar with delight when they collapsed.

The washing was folded. The kitchen wiped down. Josh's trainers sat drying by the radiator after an overenthusiastic puddle incident. There was nothing pressing to be done. That, somehow, was the problem. The house felt suspended — as though it were waiting for something to begin.

Marie stood at the window with Joseph balanced against her hip and Caleb pressing warm and insistent against her knee. The light over the bay was flat today, the sea a dull sheet of pewter. Once, she would have reached instinctively for a palette knife to catch that metallic sheen — the way grey tipped almost imperceptibly into green. Now she only noted it. She noticed the colour. Nothing more.

Caleb tugged at her leggings, impatient.

"All right," she murmured, the decision forming without ceremony. "Let's go somewhere."

The road to Hartwell curved inland, away from the sea. Without the horizon, everything felt closer. Hedges crowded the verge; the sky narrowed to a pale strip overhead. By the time they arrived, the rhythm of the car had lulled Joseph to sleep. Caleb blinked heavily from the buggy, resisting rest as if it were an insult.

Hartwell hummed in a way Brookleigh Bay never quite did. Shop doors opened and shut. Cutlery clinked against china. Conversations overlapped without meaning. No one knew her here. She was simply a woman pushing a double buggy down a high street. She paused outside a café, reading the chalkboard menu without intending to go inside. She wasn't hungry. She was drifting again.

And then she saw him.

Across the road, near a restaurant with dark green awnings, stood a man with Luke's posture — that slight forward lean, as though bracing against a wind even when there was none. She had learned that he did this to try to be the same height as other people. His weight rested on his right leg, left foot angled outward exactly as it always did when he was thinking. He wasn't in work gear. No high-vis jacket. No dust on his boots. Just a dark coat, well-cut and unfamiliar.

Marie slowed.

It isn't him. It cannot be. Luke was on site. He had texted mid-morning about a late timber delivery. A photo had followed — pallets stacked against raw brick.

The man turned slightly. The small pale notch at the edge of his ear — the scar Josh once called his "pirate bite" — caught the light.

The air left her lungs.

Beside him stood a woman. She was — Marie could not help the word — assured. Not ostentatiously beautiful. Just composed. Her hair fell in a deliberate sweep over the collar of her coat. No stains. No hurried elastic biting into her wrist. A slim leather folder rested against her side. Professional. Contained.

The man reached for the restaurant door. As the woman stepped inside, his hand hovered briefly at the small of her back — not intimate, not lingering. But familiar. Automatic.

The gesture was brief. Ordinary.

Marie felt it like a stone dropped into still water.

A bus roared between them, brakes hissing, a wall of steel and glass. When it passed, the pavement was empty. The restaurant door closed.

Gone.

You are projecting, she told herself, fingers tightening around the buggy handle. Boredom invents stories. Loneliness makes patterns where there aren't any.

Joseph stirred, soft and warm against her chest. Caleb squirmed, restless. Marie stood very still, as if the world might rearrange itself into something sensible again.

It did not.

She wandered afterwards without direction. Shop windows reflected her back at herself in fractured panels of glass. Hair pinned up in haste. Milk dried faintly at the shoulder of her jumper. The double buggy — a wide, plastic barricade between her and the world.

She looked tired.

She stopped outside an art supply shop. In the window, tubes of oil paint were arranged in a slow gradient: Naples Yellow into Cadmium, into Alizarin, into Ultramarine so deep it was almost night. A fan of sable brushes caught the light like something ceremonial.

For a moment — just a moment — she imagined walking in.

Buying the Ultramarine. Buying the Cadmium Red. Opening the wardrobe. Taking down the sketchbook.

Feeling the weight of a brush between her fingers.

Then she imagined Luke's hand at the small of another woman's back.

The image slipped in uninvited, sharp and unwelcome.

She stepped away from the window as if it had burned her.

That evening Luke came home mud-splashed and solid, the smell of damp earth and wood shavings clinging to him. He kissed her temple in passing, casual and unguarded.

"Long day," he said, voice rough with fatigue.

"Mm."

She watched him as he spoke — about brickwork, about delayed deliveries, about a subcontractor who'd mis-measured a frame.

His face was open. Familiar. Nothing hidden. Nothing secret.

She searched anyway.

The evening routine unfolded around them — dinner, baths, toys scattered across the rug. When the boys were finally wrangled into pyjamas, Luke clapped his hands lightly.

"Family Bible time, lads."

Josh ran to fetch the family Bible. Caleb toddled after him, dragging a blanket behind him like a stubborn little tail. They gathered on the sofa, Joseph on Marie's lap, Caleb wedged between his parents, Josh leaning against Luke's shoulder.

Luke opened to the bookmarked page. "Tonight we're in Psalms."

Josh settled. Caleb immediately tried to turn the pages. Luke gently moved his hand aside.

He read the verses slowly, his voice steady and warm. Marie listened, but the words felt distant, as though she were hearing them through glass.

The Lord is near to the broken-hearted...

Her chest tightened.

When Luke finished, he looked at the boys. "What do you think that means?"

Josh answered first. "It means God helps when we're sad."

Luke nodded. "And when we don't know what to do."

Marie stared at the pattern on the rug.

Caleb shouted, "God!" and threw his blanket in triumph.

Luke laughed softly. "Close enough."

They prayed together — simple, unpolished words — and then Josh leapt up. "Chocolate time!"

The boys chose their treats. Luke chose last. Marie did not choose at all.

Later, as Luke reached for her hand on his way past, the gesture was instinctive. Ordinary.

Marie felt it land differently now.

The silence between them was not dramatic. It was not hostile.

It was simply heavier than it had been that morning.

And for the first time in a long while, the house no longer felt suspended.

It felt uncertain.

Chapter 6

Monday afternoon brought a heavy, bruised sky that never quite managed to break into rain. The timber had finally arrived, but the delay had rippled through the day's schedule like a slow-motion collision. Luke stood with George at the edge of Plot 12, boots sunk into churned mud, breath misting in the cold air as they watched the first stacks of treated pine being craned onto the site.

Around them, the estate hummed with a frantic, late-shift energy. Plasterers were shouting measurements through open window frames, and electricians were threading miles of cable through skeletal walls.

"Finally," George grunted, checking his watch. "Thought they were coming from the moon, not the A19."

"At least we can get the joists in before the light goes," Luke said, rubbing the back of his neck. He had already texted Marie a quick photo of the pallets against the raw brickwork earlier that morning—a small piece of proof that he was buried in work.

By half-past one, the initial chaos had settled. Luke clapped George on the shoulder. "You've got this? I've got to head into Hartwell for that meeting."

George snorted, already waving a forklift forward. "I always do. Go on—get off before something else turns up late. I'll see you tomorrow."

Luke headed for the van, wiping his hands on a rag. He took the back road to Hartwell, arriving just as the town was settling into the quiet lull that followed the main lunch rush. The narrow streets were damp, reflecting the pale, flat light.

Amelia, the estate agent, was already waiting outside a small restaurant tucked away from the main high street. It was a place Luke hadn't visited before, marked by dark green awnings that looked crisp against the old stone. She wore a smart navy coat and carried a slim leather folder tucked neatly under her arm.

"Mr Linton?" she asked, offering a polite, professional smile as he approached.

"Luke," he corrected, shaking her hand.

"I've brought the details for the two properties we discussed," she said, gesturing toward the door. "Shall we? It's a bit quieter inside now."

They stepped into the warmth of the restaurant. It was nearly two o'clock, and most of the tables were empty. As Amelia headed for a booth near the window, Luke followed, his hand hovering briefly near the small of her back—a reflexive, polite gesture to guide her through the narrow space.

They ordered a late lunch, and Amelia spread the papers across the table. Luke leaned forward, his weight resting on his right leg, his left foot angled out as he studied the listings.

"This first one is the old shoe shop in Brookleigh Bay," Amelia explained, tapping a photograph. "It's structurally sound, though it's been empty for a year. The upstairs has wonderful light."

Luke looked at the image, but his mind was already moving further down the coast. "And the other one?"

She slid a second sheet across the table. The fisherman's shack.

Luke's pulse kicked. He knew that building—a weathered, stubborn little structure that sat just above the high-tide mark. It had been empty for five years, a wasted piece of potential. He could already picture the wide doorway opening onto the sand and the upstairs loft where the light would be perfect for a canvas.

"It only just came on the market," Amelia said. "It needs a lot of work, which is why the price is where it is."

"I'd like to see both," Luke said, his voice steady despite the rising excitement. "Friday morning? After the school run."

"I can do half-past nine," she replied, making a note in her folder.

They finished their meal, and Luke headed back to the site, the quiet hope of the studio project buzzing beneath his ribs. He spent the rest of the afternoon carrying timber, the physical strain grounding him.

By the time he walked through his front door that evening, the house smelled of dinner and soap. Josh was shouting about a goal he'd scored at break, and Caleb was dragging a blanket across the rug.

Luke leaned in to kiss Marie's temple. She stiffened—just a fraction—but he put it down to the exhaustion of a long Monday with three children.

"Long day?" he asked, reaching for Joseph.

"Mm," was all she said.

He launched into the usual report: the timber delay, the site gossip, the late lunch. Every word was technically true, yet he kept the image of the fisherman's shack tucked away, a bright secret he was building for her, piece by piece.

He didn't notice the way she was searching his face as he spoke. He did not see the shadow in her eyes that had not been there when he left that morning. He simply carried his hidden joy into the evening, unaware that the foundation he was trying to build was already beginning to crack.

Chapter 7

The café in Brookleigh Bay was warm, but it was the damp, close warmth of steamed milk and wet wool. Marie had arrived early — not from punctuality, but because the alternative was standing in the hallway while Caleb tried to eat a piece of dried mud and Joseph screamed as if he had not fed ten minutes earlier.

"Hello, Marie." Graham smiled as she walked to the corner table. She built a small fortress from the double pram and a scatter of teething rusks.

"James and Ben have taken all the kids to soft-play," Izzy announced as she swept in, her scarf a bright slash of Alizarin Crimson against the grey morning. She looked radiant — the kind of new-baby glow Marie felt had been worn thin on her own skin by sleepless nights and hurried showers. "Apparently it's 'character-building.' I think they just wanted chips at eleven in the morning."

Marie gave a small laugh. It felt brittle. "That sounds about right."

Joseph began the low, rhythmic whimper that meant escalation was imminent. She shifted him to her other hip, her back giving its usual warning twinge. Caleb lunged for her latte, sticky fingers inches from porcelain.

"Careful, Caleb." She intercepted him automatically — the reflex of someone who had prevented a thousand small catastrophes.

Julie arrived moments later, hair still damp from the school run, cheeks flushed with movement and purpose.

"I dropped off my return-to-work forms on the way," she said, sliding into the seat opposite. "Two more weeks, then I'm back in the classroom."

"You must be thrilled," Izzy said.

"I am," Julie admitted. Her eyes held a spark Marie could not remember seeing in her own reflection. "It'll be good to use my brain again. To talk about something other than *Bluey* and nap schedules."

Use my brain again.

The words settled heavily.

Marie looked down at Joseph, his head a soft weight against her chest. She loved the milk-sweet smell of him. But in that moment she felt herself thinning around the edges. She was not an artist. She was not even Marie.

She was a pair of hands.

A source of milk.

A manager of laundry.

"Marie?" Julie's voice gentled. "You're quiet today. Is everything all right? Is Luke okay?"

The name moved through her like cold air.

Green awnings.

A dark coat.

A hand at the small of a polished back.

"Just tired," she said, lifting her usual smile into place. "Caleb was up twice. And Joseph is... Joseph."

It was not untrue.

It just was not the thing pressing at her ribs.

They talked about Izzy's final exams for her counselling qualification and Julie's timetable. Marie nodded at the right places, checked Caleb's nappy, bounced Joseph gently. But it felt as though she were watching from the opposite bank of a wide river — one that moved too quickly to cross.

They were stepping back toward classrooms and studios and offices. She was still standing on the shore.

The wind off the sea was sharp when they left — a deep Prussian Blue cold that cut clean through her coat. She pushed the heavy double pram along the coastal path, wheels clicking against uneven pavement.

She thought of the woman in Hartwell again. That woman probably didn't have dried porridge at her collar. She probably did not feel transparent in her own kitchen.

At home, the house greeted her with its familiar hum. She hung coats, settled the boys, moved through the necessary small tasks. Then she stood in the centre of the kitchen.

Her hands trembled — just slightly.

She looked at the laundry basket.

At the kettle.

At the door Luke would walk through in a few hours, carrying cold air and sawdust and something she could not name.

The kettle clicked off. She did not remember switching it on.

Marie pressed her palms against the cool countertop.

The house smelled faintly of toast and baby shampoo — the ordinary scents of a life she had once entered with joy. Now they felt like instructions: *Be grateful.*

She was grateful.

That did not quiet the hollow ache.

A soft thud sounded from the living room — Caleb dropping a toy. Joseph gave a sleepy sigh from the sling.

Life continued, steady and unaware.

Her gaze drifted back to the door.

Luke would come in later, brushing cold from his shoulders. He would kiss the boys. He would kiss her, too — if she let him. And she would stand there, trying to read meaning into the angle of his body, the steadiness of his eyes.

She poured water into a mug and watched the steam rise, blurring the dark window until her reflection softened into someone she almost recognised.

Who was that woman in Hartwell?

The question throbbed quietly.

She tried to pray — something simple, something steady — but the words dissolved before they formed.

A car door slammed outside.

Her body tightened before her mind could reason. Too early for Luke. Probably a neighbour.

Still, she set the mug down, untouched.

The boys murmured in their sleep. The fridge hummed. The wind tapped at the letterbox.

Marie stood very still and realised she did not know how she would meet Luke tonight — with trust, with questions, or with the careful smile she had been practising all morning.

Chapter 8

Sunday mornings at Brookleigh Bay Community Church usually had a rhythm that steadied her — a tide that carried her gently back toward centre.

Today the tide felt heavier.

"Ready?" Luke asked, already balancing Caleb under one arm while tightening the strap on Joseph's car seat with his free hand. "We'll miss the first hymn if we don't move."

"I'm ready," Marie said.

The mirror in the hallway suggested otherwise: pale, a faint smear of Joseph's breakfast at her collar.

The walk up the hill was brisk. Josh ran ahead, coat flaring behind him like a cape. Luke pushed the double pram with easy strength, making its weight look incidental.

Marie watched the back of his head, the steady rhythm of his stride, and felt a swell of love so sharp it almost hurt.

He's here, she reminded herself. He's right here.

The foyer was a familiar chaos of coffee steam, damp umbrellas, and the worship band warming up in uncertain keys.

"Morning, Lintons!" Lorna — Pastor Mark's wife — stood by the welcome table, clay faintly lining the creases of her fingernails, the quiet proof of the pottery studio she refused to relinquish. She squeezed Marie's arm gently. "You look like you need a week's sleep, love."

"Or a year," Marie said. Inside, the service began.

Ten minutes in, Joseph started the thin, warning cry that signalled hunger or fatigue or both. Marie reached for the changing bag, shoulders tightening, but Luke was already rising.

"I've got him," he murmured, his breath warm at her ear.

He carried Joseph to the back, settling into the slow side-to-side sway he had perfected over two babies. His large hand covered most of Joseph's back, steady and sure.

Marie sat in the pew with her lap suddenly light.

At the front, Pastor Mark turned to Ecclesiastes.

"There is a time for everything... a time to tear down and a time to build."

The words lingered.

Marie looked at Luke. He was gazing up at the timber roof-trusses, his expression thoughtful. She could not tell whether his mind was on the school extension — or somewhere else entirely.

During the final hymn, Lorna slipped into the pew beside her. "The offer still stands," she said softly. "The pottery studio. An hour to yourself. No one needs you there."

Marie swallowed. "Thank you."

Afterwards, Ben and James were recounting soft-play injuries to the coffee queue with dramatic flair.

"Two socks lost," James announced. "And I'm fairly sure my dignity is still in the ball pit."

Laughter rippled around them.

Luke returned Joseph — now sleeping — into Marie's arms. His eyes were warm, open, tired. So open she felt the sting of sudden shame.

How could I doubt him?

"Let's walk to the park for ten minutes," Luke suggested as they stepped back into the February air. "Josh needs to burn off that biscuit."

Robbie came with them, and Ben said he would pick him up later. They moved along the coastal path, Caleb asleep in the pram, Josh and Robbie darting ahead. The sea was restless but familiar, the sky a thin wash of blue.

Luke's hand brushed hers as they walked — small, unconscious, steady.

She wanted to lean into it.

Wanted to let the morning settle her.

She was almost sure it had not been him in Hartwell.

Almost sure their life was enough.

Almost steady again.

But as the North Sea wind pressed cold against her face, she realised that *almost* was a very lonely place to stand.

Chapter 9

Friday morning arrived with a thin mist clinging to the rooftops, softening the edges of the town. Luke loaded Josh into the van, the school bag thumping against the passenger footwell.

"You'll be there at three?" Josh asked, fastening his seatbelt with the solemnity of a much older child.

"I said I would, didn't I?" Luke ruffled his hair. I'll be right there at the gate."

Josh nodded, satisfied.

After dropping him at the school gates, Luke drove toward the high street, the van heater humming against the chill. His stomach fluttered with a nervous excitement he had not felt in years — not since he had first asked Marie out, not since he had proposed.

He wanted this to be right. More than right — he wanted it to be hers.

Amelia was already waiting outside the old shoe shop, clipboard in hand, her breath forming small clouds in the air. "Morning, Luke," she said. "Shall we take a look?"

They stepped inside. Dust motes drifted lazily in the slanted light. The space was small but bright, with a wide front window that looked out onto the street. The upstairs room had a pitched ceiling and a single skylight.

"It wouldn't take much," Amelia said. "New roof, new electrics, a bit of plastering."

Luke nodded, running a hand along the window frame. "She'd like the light."

He could picture Marie standing here, brush in hand, the morning sun catching the copper strands in her hair. He could picture her talking to customers, smiling in that quiet way she used to when she was proud of something she had made.

The space felt contained.

Safe, yes.

Predictable.

Marie had never been predictable.

"Let's see the other one," he said.

The fisherman's shed sat just above the beach, stubborn against the wind, its weathered boards silvered by years of salt and sun. The sea murmured below, restless and familiar. Luke's heart lifted.

"This one needs more work," Amelia warned as she unlocked the door. "Quite a lot more."

He stepped inside.

The air smelled of old rope and seaweed. The floorboards creaked. The walls bowed slightly, as though the building were leaning into the wind.

But the light —

The light was extraordinary.

A wide window faced the water, the whole room washed in a soft, shifting glow. Upstairs, the loft space opened into a slanted ceiling with a north-facing window that framed the horizon like a painting.

Luke stood very still.

He could see it.

He could see *her* here.

The colours she would mix.

The canvases she would fill.

The way she might breathe differently in a space that belonged to her again.

"I want to put in an offer," he said quietly.

Amelia blinked. "On this one?"

"Yes. I want to put in an offer on this shack."

She nodded, already pulling out the paperwork. "I'll submit it today and let you know what the vendors say."

Luke signed where she indicated, his signature firm, decisive. A small thrill ran through him — the feeling of building something that mattered.

By the time he reached the school gates at three o'clock, the rain had settled into a steady drizzle. Josh spotted him immediately and ran over, coat hood bouncing.

"You came!"

"Told you I would." Luke tousled his hair. "How was your day?"

Josh launched into a story about a spelling test and a football game that had ended in a disputed goal. Luke listened, smiling, the offer on the fisherman's shed glowing quietly in his chest.

Back on site, the rain had worsened. The joiners were packing up, the plasterers already gone, and George was locking the container.

"Washout," George said, shaking his head. "No point staying."

Luke nodded. "Yes. Go home. I'll see you Monday."

George paused, eyeing him. "So? How'd your mysterious meeting go?"

Luke hesitated — then told him everything. About the shoe shop. About the shed. About the light. About Marie.

George's grin spread slowly. "You daft romantic. She'll love it."

"I hope so," Luke said quietly.

"You're doing a good thing," George replied. "You always do."

Luke felt the words settle warm in his chest.

He spent the rest of the afternoon at home. The house smelled of tomato sauce and warm bread. Caleb ran toward him, arms outstretched, and Luke scooped him up with a grin.

Marie was at the counter, stirring a pot with one hand while balancing Joseph on her hip. She looked up as he entered.

"Hi," she said.

Her voice was soft. Too soft.

Luke crossed the kitchen and kissed her cheek. She did not pull away, but she did not lean in either.

"Tired?" he asked. "Do you want me to take Joseph?"

"Okay."

He wanted to tell her everything — about the shoe shop, about the shed, about the way the light had caught the sea through that wide window. But she looked worn, stretched thin around the eyes, and he did not want to add anything heavy to her day.

So he kept it to himself.

Over dinner, he told the usual stories — the timber delivery, the joiners, the architect who had finally sent the revised plans. Marie nodded in the right places, smiled faintly, but her gaze drifted more than once.

He did not notice.

Not really.

He was too busy turning the fisherman's shed over in his mind, piece by piece, imagining how he would make it ready for her.

Later, after the boys were in bed and the house had settled into its evening quiet, Luke stood at the kitchen window, looking out at the dark curve of the bay.

He felt hopeful.

He felt purposeful.

He felt like he was building something that mattered.

Upstairs, Marie lay awake, staring at the ceiling, the image of the man in Hartwell — the coat, the posture, the hand at the small of the woman's back — flickering behind her eyes.

Two people in the same house.

Two hearts moving in different directions.

Neither of them knew it yet.

Chapter 10

It was Lorna who suggested the trip.

"Come on," she said, looping her arm through Marie's. "Fresh air. A wander. Coffee. Nothing serious."

Marie agreed. She liked being with Lorna — her unhurried presence, her refusal to pry. After the unsettled days of the past week, stepping outside felt like loosening a knot.

They spent an hour in the craft shop, Caleb asleep in the pram while Lorna selected tools for her studio. They shared a pastry in a café and talked about glaze colours and school newsletters and nothing that pressed too hard.

They looked in a few dress shops and Marie waited while Lorna tried on some dresses. In the end, even though Marie told her when they looked nice, she did not buy any. For a while, Marie felt almost steady again.

On the walk back toward the car park, the sky had bleached into a pale, brittle blue. The high street buzzed — a delivery van reversing, someone arguing cheerfully about takeaway options, the bank doors swinging open and shut.

Lorna slowed mid-sentence.

"Oh," she said quietly. "Isn't that Luke?"

Marie followed her gaze. Across the street, outside a glass-fronted office building, stood Luke. No work boots. No high-vis. Just jeans and a dark jacket. He looked composed. Intent.

Beside him stood a woman. Her coat fitted cleanly. Her neatly brushed hair fell in a deliberate sweep. A folder rested against her side while she gestured toward a set of papers, explaining something with calm assurance.

Luke listened closely. Nodded once. Asked a question. The woman laughed — a brief, easy sound. Luke smiled in return. Not flirtatious. Not careless. Engaged.

Marie's grip tightened on the pram handle.

Lorna's fingers brushed her arm. "Marie?"

The woman motioned toward the building entrance. Luke followed her inside without hesitation. The door closed.

Marie stood very still.

"I'm sure there's a reason," Lorna said gently.

"Of course," Marie replied. Her voice sounded distant to her own ears. "It must be work."

But Luke did not work in this town. And he had not mentioned coming here.

Lorna glanced at her. "Do you want to go over?"

"No." The word came quickly. Too quickly. "No, I don't want to... interrupt."

Interrupt what? She did not know. She did not want to frame it in words.

They lingered a moment longer, the street suddenly too loud, too bright.

Then Marie adjusted the pram and forced a small smile. "We should head back."

Lorna hesitated, then nodded.

They walked toward the car park, but Marie's thoughts stayed behind — in that doorway, with that quiet exchange, with Luke's attentive expression. She told herself she trusted him. That she knew him.

As they reached the car and Caleb stirred in his sleep, Marie glanced back down the street. The glass doors remained closed. Luke did not reappear.

And the space where certainty had once sat felt wider than before.

Chapter 11

Luke had not meant to come back into town that afternoon. He told himself he had too much on — the timber delivery, the school extension, the endless list of jobs that came with running two sites at once. Monday should have been a day for catching up, not adding more to his plate.

But ever since Friday, the fisherman's shack had been sitting under his ribs like a live thing.

He had walked through the shoe shop politely, listening to Amelia's explanations about rooflines and footfall and potential. It was fine. Sensible. Practical.

But the shack...

The shack had felt like possibility.

He could still see it: the salt-bleached boards, the stubborn little doorway, the upstairs loft with its slanted ceiling and that window — the one that caught the sea light in a way that made him think of Marie's old canvases. The ones she used to paint before the boys, before the exhaustion, before the colour drained out of her days.

He had put in an offer on Friday morning. Lower than he wanted, lower than the place deserved, but all he could justify with the amount of work it needed. He'd told Amelia he understood if the vendor refused. He'd told himself he could wait.

By Monday lunchtime, he knew he could not.

He kept checking his phone between tasks, half-expecting it to buzz in his pocket. It did not. Not once. By early afternoon, the not-knowing had become a restless ache.

He wanted this for Marie.

He wanted it so badly it frightened him.

So he drove into town.

He told himself it was practical — a quick conversation, a simple check-in. But the truth was simpler: he was excited, and he wanted to know. He wanted to hold the news in his hands, good or bad, instead of letting it churn inside him.

Amelia was just leaving the office when he arrived, her folder tucked neatly under her arm. She looked surprised, then smiled.

"Luke. I wasn't expecting you."

"I know," he said, rubbing the back of his neck. "I just wondered if you'd heard anything. About the shack."

Her expression softened. "Not yet. The vendor's been slow to respond. I was going to ring you as soon as I heard."

"Right." He nodded, trying to hide the disappointment. "I just thought... well. I thought I'd check."

She opened the folder, flicking through the papers. "Your offer is fair, considering the work needed. If they're sensible, they'll take it. But I'll chase them again now."

"Thanks. I appreciate it. If it needs to be increased, could you increase it by £50 a time and let me know when they accept?"

They stood outside the office, talking through the practicalities — surveys, timelines, the likely cost of repairs. Amelia laughed once at something he said about the roof joists, and he smiled back, distracted, his mind already in that loft room with the sea light pouring in.

She gestured toward the office door. "Come in for a minute. I'll make the call now and if they don't accept this offer, I will do as you say but let you know each time."

He followed her inside.

He did not see the street.

He did not see the pram.

He did not see Marie.

He only felt the fragile hope he'd been carrying all weekend — the hope that this might be the thing that helped her breathe again.

He was halfway back to the van when his phone buzzed.

Amelia.

He stopped walking, breath catching in the cold air.

"Luke? It's good news," she said, a smile audible in her voice. "The vendor has accepted your offer. They're happy to move quickly if you are."

For a moment he could not speak. Relief and disbelief washed through him in one sharp, bright rush.

"That's... that's brilliant," he managed. "Thank you. Really. Thank you."

"We'll get the paperwork moving," Amelia said. "I'll email everything over this afternoon."

He ended the call and stood there, phone still in his hand, the winter light catching on the windscreen of his van. The fisherman's shack. Marie's studio. A place she could breathe again. It was happening. It was actually happening.

He wanted to tell her.

He wanted to see her face when she realised what he'd been trying to build for her.

But not yet.

Not until it was certain.

Not until he could put the keys in her hand.

Luke climbed into the van, heart thudding with a quiet, rising joy he had not felt in months.

He did not know that across the street, Marie had already seen him walk inside with Amelia.

He did not know how much that moment would cost them both.

Chapter 12

Saturday mornings at the library were one of Marie's small, steady rituals. Josh loved story hour, and Luke had offered — without hesitation — to stay home with Joseph and Caleb.

"You two go," he had said, kissing the baby's head. "We'll have a boys morning."

So Marie and Josh walked hand-in-hand beneath a pale winter sky. Inside the library, warmth wrapped around them — children sprawled on beanbags, parents murmuring softly, Mrs Gable shelving books with her usual quiet efficiency.

"Josh!" Robbie Carter skidded around the corner, his hearing aids clearly visible today, nearly dropping his stack of books. Julie followed at a more sensible pace, baby in a sling.

"Thought we might see you," Julie said with a smile. "Before these two disappear — I'm supposed to inform you Robbie now prefers Rob or Robert. Apparently, it's more mature."

"It is," Rob insisted. "And I'm not a baby."

Marie nodded solemnly. "Rob it is."

The boys disappeared towards the children's section, already debating the merits of the new Bright Sparks game.

Marie and Julie were mid-conversation when the sharp click of heels cut across the wooden floor — too loud, too deliberate for a Saturday morning library. Then came the perfume. Floral. Heavy.

Hilary Dalton appeared at the end of the aisle, crime novels tucked against her chest.

"Well," she said, smile lingering a fraction too long. "If it isn't Marie Linton."

Julie's posture shifted — polite but braced.

"Morning, Hilary," Marie said evenly.

Hilary stepped closer, lowering her voice in theatrical confidence. "I couldn't help noticing something the other day."

Marie held her gaze. "Oh?"

"Your Luke," Hilary continued lightly. "He's been in Hartwell. Twice now. With a rather beautiful woman."

The words landed with quiet precision. Julie stiffened beside her.

Marie kept her expression steady. "I'm sure it was work."

"Perhaps." Hilary tilted her head. "She's striking. Dark hair. Immaculate coat. The sort of woman who draws attention."

She paused, watching.

"And Luke looked very attentive."

Marie felt something tighten beneath her ribs.

"I assumed you knew who she was," Hilary added. "But perhaps not."

Silence hung between them — thick, uncomfortable.

"I'm sure there's nothing in it," Marie said carefully.

Hilary's smile deepened — not cruel, exactly. Interested. "If you say so."

She moved away, heels clicking softly this time, perfume trailing behind her.

Julie exhaled. "Ignore her. She thrives on stirring things."

Marie nodded. Twice. The word echoed more loudly than Hilary's tone had.

On the walk home, Josh and Rob talked endlessly about their books, but Marie barely followed the thread. Her mind circled the same images, now sharpened by confirmation.

Luke's attentive expression.

The woman's measured confidence.

Hilary's knowing smile.

When she reached the front door, she paused for a breath before stepping inside.

Luke looked up from the sofa, Caleb asleep on his chest, Joseph rolling happily on his mat. His face lit up when he saw her.

"Hey, love," he said. "Good morning?"

The scene was ordinary. Tender. Entirely unchanged.

Marie smiled back — because she loved him, because the boys were watching, because she was not ready to fracture anything yet.

But something inside her had shifted. And this time, it did not feel like something she could smooth back into place with a quiet word or a careful smile.

Chapter 13

March brought a different quality of light to Brookleigh Bay — higher, thinner, edged with the faint promise of warmth. The sea remained steel-cold, but the sky had begun to lift, as though something were shifting just out of sight.

Marie dressed Joseph slowly, fastening the tiny buttons with steady fingers. She was not sure what she hoped for from the morning — reassurance, perhaps. Or simply a place where she did not have to hold herself together quite so tightly.

Luke was already downstairs, crouched in the hallway fastening Caleb's shoes while Josh recited his memory verse with dramatic emphasis. When Marie stepped into view, Luke glanced up.

"You all right?" he asked quietly.

She met his eyes. "Ready."

It was not the whole truth.

But it was not a lie either.

The walk to church was brisk. Josh ran ahead, coat flaring behind him. Luke pushed the pram with his usual easy strength. Marie walked beside him, close enough to feel the warmth of his shoulder through their coats.

Inside, the foyer hummed — coffee steam, low conversation, lighter spring jackets replacing winter wool. Lorna caught her eye from the welcome table and offered a small, steady smile. Marie returned it.

They slid into their usual pew. Luke shifted Joseph against his shoulder; the baby's breathing was already evening out.

The first chords of the opening song rose gently through the room. Marie closed her eyes.

She did not sing. She just listened. And for a moment, she let the music hold what she had been carrying alone.

When Pastor Mark stepped forward, Bible open, his tone was unhurried.

"This morning," he said, "we're in Psalm 139. A psalm about being known."

Marie felt the word settle.

Known. Not suspected. Not misread. Not quietly unravelling. Known.

"You have searched me, Lord, and you know me," Mark read. "You perceive my thoughts from afar."

Marie stared at the grain of the pew in front of her. She thought of Hartwell. Of angled phone screens. Of questions she had not asked.

"Before a word is on my tongue," Mark continued, "you, Lord, know it completely."

Beside her, Luke shifted slightly. She glanced at him — just briefly — and saw something in his expression that had not been there a few weeks ago. Fatigue. And something gentler. Almost vulnerable. She looked away before he could notice.

During the final hymn, Luke's hand brushed against hers where it rested on the pew. Not deliberate. Not dramatic. Just contact. She did not move away.

After the service, Pastor Mark paused beside them, smiling at the boys.

"How are you both?" he asked kindly. "I hope you are well?"

Luke let out a breath — quiet, almost shaky — and nodded.

Marie felt something inside her loosen slightly. Not clarity. Not certainty. Just a softening.

As they stepped into the aisle, a familiar figure approached — Mrs Linton, coat buttoned to the top, silver hair swept neatly back. She had been helping in the crèche that morning, a smear of poster paint bright against her sleeve.

"There you are," she said, her voice warm as she reached for Caleb's hand. "I've been looking for my boys."

Caleb beamed up at her. "Nana!"

She scooped him up with the ease of someone who had lifted toddlers her whole life. Then her gaze shifted to Marie — steady, searching, not intrusive but knowing.

"You all right, love?" she asked quietly.

Marie summoned a smile. "Just tired."

Mrs Linton's eyes softened. "Yes. It's a season. They don't half take it out of you at this age." She brushed a crumb from Marie's shoulder with a gentle, mothering gesture. "But you're doing well. Better than you think. And something to help when you need it, whatever it is with children, it will pass."

The words landed with unexpected weight — not flattery, not performance, just truth spoken by someone who had lived enough life to recognise the shape of strain.

Luke came over, adjusting Joseph in the sling. His mother reached out and touched his arm. "You look done in, Luke. Make sure you rest this afternoon."

He laughed softly. "I will."

But Marie noticed the way he leaned into the touch — the boy still inside the man.

Mrs Linton turned back to her. "If you need a break this week, you tell me. I'll take the little ones. No fuss."

Marie nodded, something loosening in her chest. "Thank you."

"Always," Mrs Linton said simply.

On the walk home, the wind had eased. The light felt different — still pale, but no longer brittle. Josh ran ahead. Caleb narrated something to himself from the pram. Joseph slept.

Luke walked close enough that their arms brushed now and then. Neither of them spoke. But the silence no longer felt like a wall.

It felt — tentatively — like space.

Chapter 14

It arrived on a Thursday morning.

The house was unusually quiet. Caleb slept upstairs. Josh was at school. Luke had left before sunrise, pressing a soft kiss to her forehead.

"Big day today," he had murmured.

Marie had been wiping down the kitchen counters when the letterbox clattered. She dried her hands and stepped into the hallway. A single white envelope lay on the doormat. Thick paper. Heavy. Her stomach tightened before she bent to pick it up.

Mr Luke Linton

Brookleigh Bay

Their address printed neatly beneath. And in the top corner, small and precise: *Harper & Cole Solicitors.*

The word seemed to alter the temperature of the hallway. *Solicitors.*

Her fingers tightened around the envelope.

It was not addressed to her. Luke would never open her post. She knew that. She also knew he had been leaving early. Returning late. Taking calls in the hallway.

Why would a solicitor be writing to him?

Why had he not mentioned it?

Marie stood there longer than she meant to, the envelope weighty in her hand. She placed it carefully on the hall table. Then stepped back. Tried to walk away.

She did not.

Her eyes returned to it.

Harper & Cole, Solicitors.

Hartwell.

The thought came uninvited. She pressed her palm lightly to her mouth, steadying her breathing.

She did not open it.

But she did not move far from it either.

Luke came home close to ten. Dust clung to his cuffs. His smile was tired but genuine.

"Hey, love," he said softly, toeing off his boots. "Sorry. It's been a day."

"There's post for you," she said.

Her voice sounded almost normal.

He glanced towards the hall table. And for the first time in weeks, something crossed his face before he caught it. Surprise. Then composure.

"Oh." He picked up the envelope, turning it over once. "Right."

He did not open it.

He did not explain.

He slipped it into his jacket pocket.

"Let me get cleaned up," he said, brushing a quick kiss against her cheek.

The bathroom door closed upstairs. Marie stood in the hallway, listening to the pipes rattle faintly in the walls.

Something was happening.

Not imagined.

Not invented.

Real.

And for the first time, the question was not whether she should ask.

It was whether she was ready for the answer.

Chapter 15

Luke had not meant to leave before sunrise, but the school extension inspection was booked for eight, and he wanted to be back early enough to help with tea.

He had kissed Marie's forehead in the half-dark.

"Big day today," he had whispered.

She murmured something soft and half-asleep in return.

He had smiled all the way to the van. The fisherman's shack was his barring the paperwork. The solicitor had called late the previous afternoon to confirm the details of the sale that would need to be processed.

Luke had stood in the empty school corridor, dust on his boots, heart thudding with a kind of reckless joy he had not felt in years. He had been very clear — send all correspondence to the company address. Nothing to the house.

He wanted to tell Marie properly. He wanted to walk her down the coastal path at dusk, hand her the keys, open the door and say — *This is yours. This is where you get to breathe.*

So, when he came home and saw the envelope on the hall table, his stomach jolted.

Not guilt. Just timing.

"Oh," he had said lightly. "Right. Thanks."

He had slipped it into his jacket pocket without opening it. Not secrecy — not really. He just did not want the moment reduced to paperwork and hallway lighting. He wanted space. He wanted surprise.

Upstairs in the shower, he rehearsed versions of the words. I bought you somewhere to paint. I want you to have something that's yours. I see you.

He imagined her shoulders loosening. The way her voice used to change when she talked about colour — how it sharpened, brightened. He imagined paint under her fingernails again.

He dried off quickly, pulled on a clean T-shirt, and headed downstairs, ready.

But Marie was wiping down the counters, movements quiet and measured. Her smile, when she looked up, was there — but muted.

He paused in the doorway. Something felt delicate.

He crossed to her, wrapped his arms around her waist.

"Long day," he murmured. "But a good one."

She leaned into him.

Briefly.

Luke tightened his hold without meaning to. Maybe she was tired. Maybe he should wait. Make it special.

He released her gently, telling himself he would choose the right moment.

Soon.

Chapter 16

By Monday, Marie had almost convinced herself the late nights were temporary — a job running over, a deadline, something practical. On Tuesday, she woke to the sound of the front door closing. Her eyes flew to the clock. 6:12 a.m. Luke was never gone before seven.

Her phone glowed on the bedside table.

5:58 a.m.

Luke: Early start today, love. Didn't want to wake you. See you tonight. xx

Marie exhaled. Of course he had told her. He always did.

Still, the house felt subtly altered — as though someone had shifted the furniture half an inch and she could not quite place what was wrong.

Downstairs, his mug sat on the counter. Tea still faintly warm. He had left quickly.

It's nothing, she told herself. He's busy. Don't build a story.

But the ache beneath her ribs tightened anyway.

She thought of their first year of marriage. Of the small flat above the chip shop. Of Josh arriving sooner than planned. Of art school quietly folding itself away. Luke had never said he felt trapped. Not once.

But sometimes, in the quiet hours, she had wondered whether love and obligation could blur into something neither of them had chosen quite so deliberately.

On Wednesday, the shower was already running when she woke. Luke came downstairs dressed, hair damp, boots on.

"You're up early," she said, aiming for lightness.

"Big job today," he replied easily. "Told you last night, remember?"

She had a faint memory of him mentioning it while she drifted toward sleep. He kissed her cheek.

"Will you be home for tea?" she asked.

"Should be. If not, I'll message."

He did.

6:34 p.m.

Running late. Sorry, love.

He arrived at half past nine, tired, apologetic. Caleb asleep. Josh long in bed.

Marie reheated his dinner, watching him eat. Love and unease sat side by side in her chest now, neither cancelling the other.

Luke reached across the table and squeezed her hand. "I know it's been a lot," he said. "It won't always be like this."

She nodded. The words slid past her without anchoring.

By Friday, the pattern had weight.

Empty bed. Early message. Late return.

Luke: Early start again. Love you.

He came home at ten, shoulders heavy, smile still there. Marie watched him remove his boots. Watched him rub his eyes. Watched him kiss her forehead as though nothing had shifted.

She wanted to trust him. She wanted to be the version of herself who didn't catalogue times and tones and subtle changes in expression. But something small had moved inside her. Not suspicion. Not accusation. Just a hairline fracture where certainty used to sit.

That night, she lay awake beside him, listening to the steady rhythm of his breathing.

The house was quiet. Familiar. And yet — in the spaces between the sounds — it felt altered. As though shadows had lengthened without her noticing.

Chapter 17

Luke sat in the cab of the van, engine idling, forehead resting briefly against the steering wheel. The street lamps cast a soft amber glow across the empty road. The town was still asleep. He should have been driving ten minutes ago. He just needed one minute when no one needed anything from him.

The exhaustion had moved past tiredness into something deeper. It sat in his joints. Behind his eyes.

Two sites. Two teams. A capable but still-settling foreman. And a fisherman's shack that required more than he had let himself calculate. He had thought he could manage it. Keep the surprise intact. Carry the weight quietly. Hand Marie the keys and watch her face change.

But the days were stretching thin. The nights shorter. And Marie — Marie was quieter. He saw it in the way she folded laundry without humming. In the way her smiles ended early. In the way she sometimes looked at him as if measuring something.

He wanted to fix it. He wanted to fix her sadness — though he knew that was not quite fair. But the only way he knew how to fix anything was to build. And he couldn't finish the shack without pushing harder.

He straightened, rubbing his eyes. The school inspection first. Then the housing site. If there was time, he'd stop at the shack and get another coat of sealant on the window frames before the rain came in from the east.

His phone buzzed.

Morning. Boys awake. Hope your day goes okay. x

He stared at the message longer than necessary. He hated these half-conversations. Early starts. Late apologies. Reassurances typed instead of spoken. It felt like withholding — even though he was withholding something good.

Love you. Big push this week. It'll settle soon. Promise. xx

He hesitated before hitting send. He hoped that was true.

By mid-morning he was ankle-deep in mud at the school site, clipboard under his arm, hard hat on his head.

"Delay on the timber," Tom said, apologetic. "Supplier's short."

Of course they were.

Luke pinched the bridge of his nose. "I'll handle it."

He should have passed it to Caroline. She handled suppliers. But every shack-related order he kept separate. Off the books she saw. Off the paper trail that might raise questions. And he could have told her — she was loyal, discreet, the safest pair of hands he had — but this was not business. This was Marie. This was the one thing he wanted to hold close until it was real. Until the keys were in his pocket. Until he could show her the space and watch her face change. Some things felt too precious to share before their time, even with people he trusted.

An hour later he had rerouted deliveries, shifted electricians, and rearranged schedules so neither site collapsed entirely.

But the shack was still behind.

He drove there anyway. The sea wind cut sharp as he unlocked the door. Inside, the space smelled of salt and old timber. Light poured in from the north-facing window — clean, steady.

He stood in the middle of the room. He could see it. An easel by the window. Shelves lined with paint. Marie standing there, sleeves pushed up, distracted in the way she used to be.

He ran a hand through his hair. He needed help. He needed to stop trying to split himself in three.

He texted George.

We need another foreman. Solid. I can't keep covering both sites.

George replied almost immediately.

I've been saying that. I'll make calls.

Luke exhaled slowly. Maybe this would ease. Maybe he could come home before dark again.

He locked up the shack, shoulders heavier than when he had arrived.

He loved his wife. He loved his sons. He loved the life they had built.

But for the first time in years, he was not certain he could hold every piece of it in place without something cracking.

Chapter 18

Lorna's pottery studio sat at the back of her shop — when Marie pushed the door open, the small bell gave a muted thud. Lorna was at the wheel, hands steady around a rising column of grey clay. The wheel hummed.

"The kettle's just boiled," she said without looking up. "Help yourself."

Marie lowered herself onto the stool by the door. Joseph slept in his carrier. Caleb fidgeted in the pushchair. The steady whir of the wheel filled the room.

"It's not work," Marie said finally.

The wheel slowed. Stopped.

Lorna wiped her hands on her apron and turned.

"The woman in Hartwell?" she asked gently.

"And the late nights. The early mornings." Marie's fingers twisted in Caleb's blanket. "And a letter from a solicitor. He put it straight in his pocket, Lorna. Like it wasn't meant for me to see."

Lorna was quiet for a moment. "Luke isn't a liar," she said carefully. "I've known him since he was sixteen. He's stubborn. He carries too much. But he doesn't lie."

"Then why does it feel like I'm standing outside my own marriage?" Marie's voice thinned. "He smiles. He kisses me. He plays with the boys. And then he steps into the hallway and closes the door."

She swallowed. "It's the normality that frightens me."

Lorna stood and crossed to a shelf of pale bisque-fired bowls — smooth, unfinished.

"When you're throwing clay," she said, lifting one gently, "sometimes there's an air pocket you can't see. From the outside, everything looks sound. But if you fire it like that, the heat will find the hollow and it'll crack." She turned the bowl in her hands. "You're holding a lot in. Questions. Fear. Imagination filling in the blanks."

Marie's eyes filled. "I feel like I'm grieving something that hasn't even happened," she whispered.

Lorna stepped closer, clay-smudged hand warm against her shoulder. "Then stop standing at the edge of it."

Marie looked up.

"Don't wait for ten o'clock and another careful conversation. Call him. Go to him. Whatever he's carrying — good or bad — you deserve to see it in daylight."

The studio was quiet again. The wheel still. Marie wiped her cheeks with the back of her hand.

For the first time in weeks, the fear felt less like fog — and more like something she could walk toward.

Chapter 19

Luke woke on Saturday with a dull ache behind his eyes. He lay still for a moment, staring at the ceiling, listening to Marie's breathing beside him.

She had drifted toward the edge of the bed again. He hated that. Hated that the week had stretched thin between them. Hated that she seemed to fold inward when he wasn't looking. He reached under the duvet and found her hand. She stirred.

"Morning," he said quietly.

She blinked at him, offering a small, tired smile.

"It's Caleb's birthday. Let's take the boys out today," he said. "All of us. No work. No errands. Just... us."

She studied him. "Really?"

"Really." He kissed her forehead. "Adventure Valley?"

Something softened in her expression. "They'll love that."

And maybe, he hoped, she would too.

Adventure Valley was already alive with noise when they arrived — shrieks from the climbing frames, the smell of coffee and hay, goats protesting loudly near the petting barn.

Josh ran ahead the moment his feet hit the gravel. Caleb clapped wildly at everything. Joseph settled against Marie's chest, content.

Luke stayed close to her. He watched her face as Josh fed the goats, as Caleb shrieked at the rabbits, as the noise and movement pressed in around them. The crease between her brows eased. Her shoulders dropped. For a few hours, she looked less guarded. He felt something loosen inside him.

"Look at him," she murmured, brushing Joseph's cheek. "He's so content."

"So am I," Luke said, and meant it.

She glanced up at him, surprised by the softness in his voice. Their eyes held for a beat — longer than they had in days.

It felt almost like before.

The playground left them breathless and laughing. Luke chased Josh up the climbing wall, scooped Caleb mid-slide, then pretended dramatic defeat when they toppled him onto the grass. Marie watched him. He looked alive. Present. Entirely himself.

And that was what made the unease harder to dismiss.

When they finally settled at a picnic bench with hot chocolates and paper-wrapped sausage rolls, Luke reached under the table for her hand.

She let him take it.

"You okay?" he asked quietly.

"It's been a good day," she said.

"It has." He hesitated. "We needed it."

He wanted to say more. *I'm trying. I haven't forgotten you. Just hold on a little longer.* But the words remained lodged somewhere behind his ribs. Instead, he squeezed her fingers.

She squeezed back. Gently.

The boys fell asleep on the drive home, one by one. The car filled with the soft rhythm of breathing and the low hum of the road.

Marie leaned her head against the window. Luke glanced at her and felt the familiar tightening in his chest. He used to pray easily. Words had come without effort. Now his mind felt crowded, restless.

Still, he whispered into the quiet of the car. "Help me."

It was simple. Bare. But it was honest.

Marie didn't hear him.

Yet something in the air between them felt less brittle than it had that morning.

Chapter 20

Sunday sunlight filtered through the stained-glass windows of Brookleigh Bay Community Church, casting muted colour across the foyer floor. The air smelled of coffee and damp coats. Children darted between pews. Familiar. Ordinary.

Marie adjusted Joseph's blanket while Caleb tugged at her sleeve. Across the room, Luke stood with Ben and James, shoulders slightly hunched, tiredness etched into his face.

"Hey, are you alive?" Ben clapped him on the back.

"Just about," Luke replied with a half-smile.

"You've missed men's breakfast three weeks running," James said lightly. "We are starting to take it personally."

Luke rubbed the back of his neck. "Work's been... heavy."

Ben's grin faded slightly. "You don't have to carry it solo, you know."

"I'm fine," Luke said. But the word felt thin.

Across the foyer, Marie saw the flicker — the brief hesitation before his smile returned.

Inside the sanctuary, the worship band began the first song. Marie settled into the pew, Caleb on her lap, Joseph warm against her chest. Luke sat beside her, his hand resting on her knee. Solid. Familiar. Still, she felt the distance.

Pastor Mark stepped forward. "How many of you slept in a bed last night?" he asked, drawing soft laughter from the room.

"And what do you need to do to sleep well?"

People shouted from the pews...

"Close your eyes."

"Lie down."

"Be still."

More laughter.

"But what if your bed had only three legs?" he continued. "Would you sleep well on a bed with only three legs? What if God kept only seventy-five percent of His promises? What if Jesus dealt with only seventy-five percent of our sin?"

The laughter faded.

"Come to me, all you who are weary and burdened," Pastor Mark said gently, "and I will give you rest."

Marie closed her eyes.

Luke stared at the floor.

"Some of you are tired in ways no one can see," Mark continued. "You show up. You smile. You keep going. But you're carrying more than you were meant to."

Luke's throat tightened. He was tired. Not just physically. Tired of splitting himself — of holding something beautiful alone. Tired of watching Marie drift without knowing how to reach her.

"Jesus doesn't say, 'Try harder,'" Mark continued. "He says, 'Come to me.'"

Luke glanced sideways at Marie. She looked steady, but her jaw was set. He reached for her hand. She let him take it. But her fingers stayed still within his.

"You don't have to be strong all the time," Mark finished. "You don't have to carry it alone."

Luke exhaled slowly. He did not know how to fix everything. But he knew this much:

He could not keep waiting for the perfect moment.

He would tell her.

Soon.

Very soon.

Chapter 21

On Sunday evening, once the boys were asleep and Marie had gone upstairs with Joseph, Luke sat at the kitchen table with a mug of tea and a stack of papers. The house was quiet. Just the hum of the fridge and the low rush of the sea beyond the promenade.

He spread out the pages he had been collecting — measurements, rough sketches, supplier quotes, notes scrawled in the margins of invoices. From the outside, the fisherman's shack looked small. Manageable.

On paper, it was anything but. He rubbed his eyes and picked up a pencil.

"Right," he muttered. "Let's be honest."

He wrote slowly, deliberately:

- Full rewire — existing system unsafe
- Replace plumbing — drainage failing
- Strip damp from two walls
- Lift and relay flooring
- Insulate roof — no draughts
- Bathroom fit-out — shower, ventilation
- Basic kitchenette
- Shelving for canvases and storage
- Lighting — track and task lamps
- Seal window frames

He sat back. Some of this work he had already completed, so he crossed out *lift and relay flooring* and *strip damp from two walls*. But it was still more than he had first admitted to himself.

But now Tom, the foreman on the school site, was finding his feet. George could hold the housing site steady. If Luke stopped trying to be everywhere at once, it could work. He could ask Caroline in the office to hire some temporary workers.

He turned to a clean page.

End of July.

He underlined it once.

If he paced it carefully, and brought in trades for the specialist jobs, the shack could be more than usable. He pictured Marie stepping inside. The pause. The intake of breath. The way she would walk straight to the window and test the light with her hand.

That image steadied him more than the tea did.

He stacked the papers neatly. For the first time in weeks, the chaos felt structured. Not gone — but ordered.

He bowed his head briefly. "Help me do this well," he whispered.

Upstairs, a floorboard creaked. He gathered the papers and switched off the light.

Soon, he told himself.

Chapter 22

On Monday morning, Marie woke to the sound of Luke moving about the bedroom. Not rushing. Not slipping out before dawn. Just dressing. She blinked at the clock. 6:45.

"You're still here," she murmured.

Luke fastened his watch and smiled. "Thought I'd have breakfast with you."

The simplicity of it caught her off guard.

"That's... nice."

He leaned over and kissed her forehead. The gesture was familiar enough to ache.

Downstairs, the kitchen filled with the usual chaos. Luke poured cereal, buttered toast, wiped jam from Caleb's sleeve with exaggerated seriousness. He drank half a cup of tea before abandoning it to rescue Joseph from tipping his bowl over.

He laughed. He lingered. He looked — not rested — but present. Marie watched him over the rim of her mug. Last week he had been leaving in darkness, coming home long after bedtime, voice thin with apology. Now he stood in the middle of the kitchen as if nothing had shifted.

"Big day?" she asked, trying to sound casual.

"Busy," he said, pulling on his boots. "But manageable."

The word lingered. *Manageable.*

He kissed her cheek before stepping outside. "Home for tea."

She nodded. The door closed. The house felt quieter than it had ten minutes earlier.

The day moved in its usual loops — school run, laundry, Joseph's nap, Caleb's endless commentary on the world. But Marie felt slightly misaligned, as though something had been nudged and not quite reset.

She found herself glancing at the clock. Then at her phone. Then back at the clock.

At half past four, her phone buzzed.

On track. Home for tea. x

She stared at the message. He was trying. She could see that. But trust, once unsettled, didn't snap back into place simply because someone was smiling again.

When he walked through the door just after six, she would greet him. She would kiss him. She would ask about his day.

And beneath it all, the quiet question would remain. Not loud. Not accusing.

Just there.

Chapter 23

On Tuesday morning, Marie bundled Joseph into the pram, wrestled Caleb into his coat, and walked the familiar route to church for ladies' Bible study. The sky was pale and thin, holding rain somewhere behind it. The air was soft against her face. She used to arrive looking forward to these mornings.

Now, as she pushed open the church hall door, her stomach tightened. Inside, the radiators clanked. The kettle hissed. The faint sweetness of biscuits hung in the air. Tables were arranged in a horseshoe, Bibles open, notebooks ready.

Lorna waved. "Morning, Marie. Sit with us."

Marie smiled — grateful and uneasy in equal measure — and settled into a chair. Joseph's car seat rested at her feet. Caleb headed straight for the toy box.

The room filled quickly with familiar laughter. And yet Marie felt slightly out of step, as though everyone else had arrived prepared and she had missed a memo somewhere.

When the study began, Lorna read from Matthew. Pens scratched against paper. Someone underlined a phrase. Another woman nodded thoughtfully and offered an insight that drew quiet murmurs of agreement.

Marie listened. The words made sense — she understood them — but they didn't anchor anywhere. They drifted past without catching.

"Any thoughts on that, Marie?" someone asked gently.

Her heart jumped.

"Oh — I'm not sure," she said quickly. "I'm still thinking."

Kind smiles. A nod. The discussion moved on. But heat lingered in her cheeks. She was not afraid of these women. She trusted them.

So why did she feel as though she had been called to the front of a classroom without revision notes?

They speak so easily, she thought. They seem certain. And I can barely keep my thoughts straight.

Joseph stirred softly. Caleb clattered plastic blocks together. She tried to breathe slowly.

When the study ended, conversations spilled into small clusters — school pickups, meal plans, holiday dates.

Lorna touched her arm. "You were quiet today."

"Just tired," Marie replied.

Lorna's gaze held hers for a moment. "You don't have to have something profound to say every week. Sometimes listening is enough."

Marie swallowed. "I feel like I've lost my footing," she admitted quietly.

Lorna's expression softened. "Then you're in the right place. None of us stand steady all the time."

Outside again, the air felt cooler. Marie told herself she belonged there. That she didn't need to perform certainty in order to have faith.

Still, as she walked home, the unease followed her — not loud, not dramatic. Just persistent. She wasn't sure when she had started feeling like an outsider in her own life.

Chapter 24

As Easter approached, the rhythm of life shifted almost imperceptibly. The mornings grew brighter and the evenings lingered longer. Luke was coming home before the boys went to bed. They had time for the family Bible reading. He wasn't suddenly carefree — the tiredness still lived in his eyes — but something in him had settled.

Marie noticed before he said anything. He listened when Josh talked. He stayed at the table after dinner. He didn't reach automatically for his phone. She wondered if he had stopped seeing the other woman.

One afternoon, folding laundry at the dining table, Marie noticed the peeling paint along the skirting board. It wasn't urgent. Just something small. She found herself thinking, *Maybe he could fix that now he's home more.* Not because she wanted more from him. But because asking felt like inviting him back in.

She made a short list:

- Loose skirting board in the hallway
- Wobbly shelf in the airing cupboard
- Dripping tap downstairs
- Coat hook fallen off
- Cupboard door that never shut properly

When she handed it to him that evening, she felt unexpectedly shy.

"Only when you've got time," she added quickly.

Luke scanned it and smiled. "These are easy. I'll get Josh to help."

"Josh?"

"He's old enough to learn a few things." He glanced toward the living room. "And I haven't been around as much as I should have."

The admission was quiet. Unadorned. Something warm shifted in her chest.

On Saturday, the house filled with the steady sounds of fixing. Josh followed Luke from room to room, wielding a plastic screwdriver with fierce concentration. Luke showed him how to check if something was level, how not to over-tighten a screw, how to steady a board before hammering.

"Is that straight?" Josh asked.

"Let's check together."

Caleb toddled behind them offering toy bricks as contributions. Joseph squealed at the noise. Marie watched from the doorway. Nothing about it was grand. No dramatic speeches. No sweeping gestures. Just Luke kneeling beside his sons, patient and present.

When the tap finally stopped dripping, Josh clapped. "We did it!"

Luke grinned. "We did."

Marie felt her throat tighten. This was what she had missed — not perfection, just presence.

Later, when the tools were put away and the boys were settled, Luke stepped close and brushed a strand of hair from her face.

"Feels good to sort things," he said.

"It does," she replied.

And for a few hours, the ache eased.

But that night, lying in the dark, the quiet questions returned. He was lighter. He was home more. He was trying. And yet she still didn't know what had pulled him away in the first place.

She turned onto her side, watching the steady rise and fall of his chest.

Please let this last, she prayed silently.

And beneath the prayer, another thought lingered:

Please let there be nothing left to uncover.

Chapter 25

The Easter holidays arrived with brighter mornings and air that finally hinted at spring. For the first time in months, Luke felt as though something had eased. The school was ahead of schedule. The housing estate was steady. Tom no longer needed him hovering. There was room to breathe.

Josh had been asking for days to "come to work with Daddy," so on Tuesday morning Luke packed snacks, a juice bottle, and Josh's little tool belt, and they set off together. Josh practically vibrated with importance.

"Are we building a whole house today?"

"Not today," Luke said. "But you can help."

That was enough.

The housing estate stood in layers — finished homes with curtains in the windows, others still skeletal and raw. Luke showed Josh the completed kitchens, the fitted skirting boards.

"Remember the one we fixed at home?" Luke said.

Josh nodded proudly in his hard hat. "With the long nails!"

"That's right."

They moved into a house still mid-plaster. The air smelled chalky and damp. Luke crouched and handed Josh a small trowel.

"Smooth strokes," he said.

Josh pressed too hard. The plaster dipped.

Luke smiled. "Good start. Takes practice."

Josh beamed anyway.

At the school site, scaffolding wrapped the new extension. Luke lifted Josh to see through the open frame.

"This is the new art room," he said. "Big windows."

Josh pressed his palms to the sill. "Mummy would like that."

Luke felt the words land somewhere deep.

"She would," he said.

The fisherman's shack was their final stop.

Josh stared at the weathered building. "Is this one yours too?"

"Sort of," Luke said, unlocking the door. "It's a special one."

Inside, the space had changed. Fresh insulation lined the roof. New electrical sockets had been installed, and the overhead lights were adjustable. The windows were sanded smooth, waiting for sealant.

Josh walked slowly, touching everything.

"What's it going to be?"

Luke hesitated just a beat.

"A place for someone to make things."

"Like you?"

"Different things."

Josh nodded solemnly. "Blue paint."

Luke laughed. "We'll see."

He stood back and looked at the room — stripped, hopeful, unfinished.

It felt closer now.

Josh fell asleep on the drive home, tool belt still strapped on. Luke glanced over and felt something settle in his chest. Not perfection. Not finished. But forward.

He just hoped Marie would feel it too.

Chapter 26

Marie knew something had shifted the moment they walked through the door. Josh burst in first, flushed and breathless.

"Mummy! I plastered a wall! And I saw the art room! And Daddy let me hold a real trowel!"

Luke followed, lifting Josh when the excitement finally tipped into sleepiness. His face was bright in a way she hadn't seen in months. She knelt to unfasten the tiny tool belt, noticing a small piece of salt-crusted wood tucked into one of the pouches.

"You must be exhausted," she said.

"I'm a builder now," Josh declared.

"Apprentice," Luke corrected, smiling.

There was an ease between them—the kind that comes from shared hours, not just shared space. Marie felt it wrap around her.

Later, after baths and bedtime negotiations, the house settled. She found Luke in the kitchen emptying the dishwasher, the quiet clink of plates the only sound in the room.

"He had a good day," she said.

"He did." He stacked the last of the side plates. "So did I."

She leaned against the counter opposite him. "You seem... different," she said carefully.

He didn't deflect. "I was pushing too hard," he admitted. "Trying to keep everything steady. If I worked more, fixed more, planned more—it would all feel secure."

"And did it?"

"No." A small exhale. "It just made me tired."

She studied him. "You felt far away," she said quietly.

His jaw tightened slightly. "I didn't mean to."

"I know."

The clock ticked between them. This was the moment, she realised. The place where she could ask the question that had lived beneath everything. *Who was she? What were you hiding? Why the solicitor?* The words rose.

She looked at him—really looked. There was effort there. And weariness. And something unresolved. But not deception. Not that. Instead, she reached for his hand.

"Josh adored today," she said.

Luke's grip tightened around hers. "I've missed too many days."

"And the others?"

"And you," he said, voice low.

The intensity of it startled her. He stepped closer and kissed her forehead—slow, deliberate, present. "Things are going to be better," he said. "I'm making sure of it."

She didn't ask how. Not yet. But as she lay in bed that night, listening to his breathing, her uncertainty shifted. It hadn't vanished. It had changed. Now it wasn't suspicion. It was waiting

Chapter 27

The next morning, the house felt almost ordinary. Sunlight lay across the kitchen tiles in pale strips. Caleb banged a spoon against his bowl with determined enthusiasm. Joseph watched from his highchair, blinking slowly, as if deciding whether the day was worth joining.

Luke was making toast, moving around Marie with an ease that should have calmed her. He had been like this more lately — present, steadier, as though he had finally set something down. Marie wanted to let herself believe in it.

Josh slid into his seat and announced, with all the importance of a boy who had seen behind the curtain of the adult world, "Daddy, can we go back to the special place today?"

Luke's hand paused mid-spread.

Only for a second. But Marie saw it.

"The special place?" she repeated, keeping her voice light.

Josh nodded vigorously. "The little house by the sea. The one that smells like wood. Where I plastered the bit and daddy said it was a good start."

Luke coughed — half laugh, half warning. "Josh."

"What?" Josh looked between them, confused. "It's not a secret from Mum, is it? I didn't say the surprise part."

Marie's pulse lifted, sharp and sudden, like a wave hitting stone. Luke's eyes flicked to hers. Not guilty. Not caught out. Just — cornered.

"Josh," he said gently, "finish your toast."

Josh, sensing he had stepped into something adult and delicate, did as he was told. Caleb squealed and flung a piece of cereal onto the floor. Joseph banged both fists on his tray.

Marie stood very still, hands wet from rinsing a cup.

The special place. A little house by the sea. The woman. The folder. Hartwell. The calls in the hallway. The solicitor's letter.

Her mouth went dry.

Luke buttered toast with exaggerated concentration, as if the angle of the knife might solve everything.

Marie turned back to the sink. The water ran too loud. She kept her face angled away until she could trust her voice.

"Is it far?" she asked quietly, as though she were asking about a new shop in town.

Luke didn't answer immediately.

"No," he said at last. "Not far."

Marie nodded once, as if that was that. But something inside her — something tight and old — shifted. She carried the moment with her all day. Through the children's play, the trip to the park. Through Caleb's nap. Through Joseph's feeds and Josh's questions and the quiet, careful business of being needed.

Luke stayed home that afternoon, "sorting bits," he said — a cupboard hinge, a sticking door. Little domestic repairs with a steady hand. Normal, helpful things. He kept catching her eye and then looking away.

By early evening, Marie felt as though she were holding a glass of water too full, trying not to spill.

When the boys were finally in bed — Josh asleep with one arm flung dramatically over his head, Caleb curled around his favourite blanket, Joseph settled after a long feed — Marie came downstairs.

Luke was in the kitchen, wiping the counters that didn't need wiping. He looked up when she entered, and for a second the tiredness in his face sharpened into something else. Expectation. Or dread.

Marie leaned her hip against the doorway and folded her arms lightly, as if bracing against a draught. "So, Josh mentioned a place today," she said.

Luke's hands stilled on the tea towel.

Marie kept her voice calm, careful. "He called it the special place."

Luke exhaled slowly, eyes dropping to the counter. Marie waited. The kettle clicked faintly as it cooled. Somewhere outside, the sea kept moving, indifferent.

Luke looked up again. "He shouldn't have said anything."

"That's not his fault," Marie replied, gentler than she felt. "He's excited."

Luke nodded once, as if accepting the rebuke.

Marie swallowed. The words she had rehearsed in her head all day felt suddenly too sharp, too risky. She tried again, simpler.

"Is there something you're building," she asked, "that you haven't told me about?"

Luke didn't answer straight away. He stared at the tea towel in his hands and twisted it once, hard.

"No," he said — and then, because he was Luke, because he could never keep a lie in his mouth, he shook his head. "I mean... yes. There is."

Marie's stomach dipped.

Luke stepped forward as if he wanted to close the distance between them but didn't know if he was allowed. "It's not what you think," he said quickly.

Marie let out a small, humourless breath. "I don't even know what I think anymore."

That landed. She saw it register in his face — not offence, but pain.

Luke's voice softened. "Marie..."

She lifted a hand, stopping him, not unkindly. "I need you to just... tell me."

Luke stared at her for a long moment, as though weighing which version of the truth would hurt less.

Then he said, very quietly, "I bought something."

Marie's fingers went cold.

"A fisherman's shack," Luke continued, words spilling now that they'd begun. "Up by the dunes. North-facing light. It's rough. I mean — really rough. But I've been fixing it up."

Marie blinked, trying to make the words arrange themselves into something that made sense.

"A shack," she repeated.

Luke nodded. "For you."

The room seemed to tilt, gently, as though the floor had shifted under her feet.

"For me," she echoed, thinner than she intended.

Luke's eyes shone with something like relief and fear tangled together. "I wanted to surprise you. I wanted it to be... ready. I wanted it to feel like a gift instead of another half-finished project you'd have to carry."

Marie pressed her palm to the edge of the counter, steadying herself.

"So the calls," she said, voice small despite her efforts. "This lady in Hartwell. The letter from the solicitor."

Luke winced. "The solicitor's letter was for the sale. The lady in Hartwell must have been the estate agent. I didn't want anything coming to the house because I—" He swallowed. "I wanted to do this properly. I wanted to say, *I see you.* I wanted you to have something that was yours again."

Marie stared at him. A part of her wanted to laugh. A part wanted to cry. A part wanted to sit down on the kitchen floor and let the whole last two months drain out of her. Instead, what rose first was something sharp and unexpected.

"Why didn't you tell me?" she asked.

Luke's face tightened, as if he had been expecting anger but not this kind — not the quiet, bruised kind.

"Because—" he began, then stopped, honest enough not to fill the space with excuses.

Marie felt tears prick hot behind her eyes. "Do you know what it felt like?"

Luke's throat bobbed as he swallowed. "Marie..."

"It felt like you were leaving," she said, the words finally breaking free. "It felt like you were stepping out into some other life and shutting the door behind you. And the whole time you were smiling at me as if nothing had changed." Her voice shook. "I started looking for clues in your face, Luke. In how you held your phone. In where your eyes went."

Luke's eyes squeezed shut for a second. When he opened them, he looked wrecked.

"I didn't mean—" His voice broke. "I thought I was helping. I thought I was fixing it."

Marie let out a sound that wasn't quite a laugh. "You can't fix me like I'm a leaking tap."

Luke flinched, but he didn't argue. He just nodded slowly, as if taking the truth into himself.

"You're right," he said. "I'm sorry."

The apology was simple. Unprotected. Marie breathed in shakily.

"I didn't need it perfect," she whispered. "I needed you."

Luke stepped closer. Very slowly, as though approaching an animal that might bolt.

"I know," he said. "I know that now."

Marie looked at him — really looked. The tiredness, the strain, the way his shoulders had carried too much. The love in his face that hadn't changed. The fear that he had broken something while trying to mend it. She wiped at her cheek with the back of her hand.

"Can I see it?" she asked.

Luke blinked. "Now?"

Marie nodded once. "If I don't see it now, I'll spend all night imagining it. And I'm done imagining things."

Luke hesitated for a beat — practicalities running through him. "The boys—"

"I'll call Lorna," Marie said. "She'll come. She always does."

Luke's mouth tightened with gratitude he didn't speak aloud.

Chapter 28

Marie made the call with hands that still trembled. Lorna answered on the second ring, and when Marie explained, there was no surprise in her voice — only steady warmth.

"I'll be there in ten," Lorna said. "Put the kettle on."

Marie hung up and turned to Luke. His eyes were fixed on her as if he couldn't quite believe she was still standing there.

"Get the keys," she said quietly.

Lorna arrived with Mark and told them to take as long as they needed.

They walked the coastal path under a sky streaked with late light. Not sunset — the colour had already begun to drain — but a softening at the edges, a gentler grey-blue than winter ever allowed. The sea moved beside them, restless as always. Luke didn't speak much. Neither did Marie. Their silence felt different out here. Not charged. Not brittle. Just full.

When the shack came into view, it looked smaller than Marie had imagined. Weathered stone. A door that had seen storms. The shape of it huddled slightly against the wind as if it had learned, over time, to endure.

Luke stopped a few steps away. His breath came out slow. "This is it," he said, voice quiet.

Marie stared.

She had walked past this stretch of dunes a hundred times without looking up. Luke's hand hovered near hers. He didn't take it. He waited.

Marie took one step forward, then another.

Luke unlocked the door. The hinge creaked as it opened — not dramatically, just honestly, like a door that wasn't used to being opened.

Inside, the air smelled of sawdust and salt and something clean beneath it — fresh insulation, bare timber, new beginnings. The place was unfinished.

Walls stripped back. Wiring neat along the beams. A patch of plaster waiting to be sanded. A stack of boards in the corner. A single window, sanded smooth, catching the last light and turning it into something pale and generous.

Marie walked to that window without thinking. She stood there, hand resting on the sill. The light fell across her fingers. It was the kind of light she used to chase. Her throat closed.

Luke stood behind her, not touching, not intruding, as though afraid his presence might break the moment. "It's rough," he said, almost apologetically. "I wanted it further along before you—"

Marie turned. Her eyes were wet. "It's beautiful," she said, and then her voice cracked. "It's — Luke, it's beautiful."

His face crumpled with relief so immediate it startled her. He let out a breath that sounded like he had been holding it for weeks.

Marie swallowed hard. "I don't know what to do with this," she admitted, voice small.

Luke stepped closer. "Just... stand in it," he said. "Let it be yours. I don't need you to react the right way. I just wanted you to have a place where you could—" He faltered. "Where you could be Marie again."

The words landed softly and painfully.

Marie looked around the room. The bare bones. The potential. The work still to come. She thought of her sketchbook on the top shelf. The acceptance letter, creased through the middle. The years of maintenance. She pressed a hand to her chest, as if to keep herself from splitting apart.

"I wanted to hate you," she whispered.

Luke blinked. "What?"

Marie gave a wet, trembling laugh. "For a while I think I did. Not you — you. But the... not knowing." She wiped her cheek again, angry at the tears. "And now I'm standing here and I can't even hold onto the anger properly because this is—" She gestured helplessly. "This is love."

Luke's eyes filled. He nodded once, jaw tight.

"I'm sorry," he said again. "I thought I was carrying it for you. I didn't realise I was shutting you out."

Marie's breath shook. Then, very slowly, she reached for his hand and laced her fingers through his. His grip tightened like a man grabbing something he had almost lost.

"I don't want you to do that again," she said. "Don't decide things alone because you think you're protecting me."

Luke nodded. "I won't."

"And if you're tired," she continued, voice firmer now, "you tell me. You don't disappear into work and leave me with my own head."

"I will," he said, and it was not a promise dressed up nicely — it was plain and urgent.

Marie squeezed his hand.

They stood together, side by side, facing the window. Outside, the sea kept moving. Inside, the light lingered on the sill as if it had been waiting for her.

Marie breathed in — deep, slow — and for the first time in a long while, her lungs felt like they reached all the way out.

"Can we paint it?" she asked suddenly, a surprising spark in her voice. "The walls. Not tonight — obviously." She glanced at him, almost shy. "But soon. Can we choose colours together?"

Luke let out a laugh that sounded dangerously close to a sob. "Yes," he said. "Yes. Whatever you want."

Marie nodded, eyes shining, and turned back to the window.

Not healed. Not fixed. But present. And no longer alone in it.

Epilogue

The morning of the grand opening arrived bright and warm, the kind of August day that seemed made for new beginnings. The little artists' shack, once weathered and forgotten, now stood freshly painted and welcoming. Luke had hung the wooden sign above the door the evening before:

Marie's Light House — Art Studio

Colourful balloons swayed gently in the breeze outside, tied to the fence posts. Buckets of fresh flowers from the local shop lined the path, their colours bright against the summer green. Anyone walking past could see that something special was happening.

Marie paused for a moment in the doorway before the first visitors arrived. She let her eyes travel slowly around the room. The shack was pristine now. Sunlight spilled through the windows and touched every wall where her paintings hung — landscapes, quiet views of the bay, fields in changing seasons, and moments she had captured over the years. Each one held a piece of the journey that had brought her here.

And woven through all of it were the memories of how the shack itself had come back to life. The long weekends repairing the roof. Luke sanding the old beams while she painted the walls. Cups of tea balanced on paint tins. Both of them laughing when the rain came through before the roof was finished. They had built it together.

Soon the first visitors arrived. Word had travelled fast through Brookleigh Bay, and before long the little shack was filled with neighbours and familiar faces.

Ben and Julie came first, Rob darting ahead of them, already pointing at the paintings he recognised from Marie's sketchbook.

Julie hugged her tightly, eyes shining. "You did it," she whispered. "Look at this place."

James and Izzy followed, Josh and Alfie in tow. The boys made a beeline for the painting of the old shack, proudly telling anyone who would listen that they had "helped" with the renovations — which mostly meant handing Luke screws and eating biscuits. James clapped Luke on the back. "You've outdone yourself, mate."

Lorna arrived with a bouquet of wildflowers, clay still faintly dusting her fingertips. "For the studio," she said, placing them gently on the counter. "And for the woman who finally stepped back into the light." Mark stood beside her, smiling warmly, taking in the room with the quiet pride of a pastor who had prayed for this moment.

More neighbours drifted in — Mrs. Harmon from the bakery, the twins from the surf shop, old Mr. Smith who claimed he remembered the shack being built "before half of you were born." The space filled with laughter, soft conversations, and the hum of a community celebrating one of its own.

Someone bought the first painting. Then another. And another. Small red stickers began appearing beside the frames. The first painting she sold showed the shack as it had once been — worn, leaning slightly, surrounded by wildflowers. Two small figures stood beside it, working together beneath a soft summer sky.

Luke stood near the door greeting people, but every so often his eyes found Marie across the room. He had never seen her look quite like this before — a mixture of quiet pride and disbelief.

Yet there was one painting with no price beside it. It hung on the far wall, slightly apart from the others. For seven years it had sat unfinished upstairs in their house. The canvas had once been a half-finished study of the bay at dusk — a bruise-coloured sky, restless water, a horizon that refused to settle.

She had meant to go back to it. The sea had been there. The sky had been there. But the light over Brookleigh Bay — the part that made the whole thing alive — had been missing.

Now the painting was complete.

The deep evening sky softened into fading violet. The sea carried the last glow of daylight, and the light over the bay held everything together — the exact moment where day gives way to night.

Luke stepped beside her as she looked at it. "You could sell that one easily," he said softly.

Marie smiled, shaking her head. "That one isn't for sale."

She slipped her hand into his. Outside, the balloons drifted gently in the warm August breeze as more people arrived, laughter and voices spilling out of the little shack. Ben and Julie were chatting with Lorna and Mark; the boys were racing around the grass; Izzy was already planning a pottery-and-painting workshop with Marie.

Seven years earlier, the light in that painting had been missing. Now it was there. And so were they.

And God had been with them through it all.

Thank you so much for reading *The Light Between Us*. It means a great deal that you chose to spend time in Brookleigh Bay and walk with these characters through their shadows and their light.

This is the fourth book in the Brookleigh Bay series, following

- After the Wedding
- Safe Enough to Stay
- The Potter's Heart

Each story can be read on its own, but together they form a tapestry of the Brookleigh Bay community — ordinary people learning to love well, to forgive deeply, and to find hope in the quiet places where God meets us.

About the Author

Dorothy Blakemore is a retired teaching psychologist and Christian novelist who writes gentle, faith-rooted stories set in the coastal town of Brookleigh Bay. Her work explores the quiet ways God brings light, healing, and hope into ordinary lives and marriages.

She lives on the North East coast of England, where the shifting sea and the rhythm of church and family life continue to inspire her writing.

The Light Between us is published under Mustard Seed Press — a reminder that even the smallest seeds of faith can grow into something beautiful.

If you'd like to get in touch, you're warmly welcome to email me at **dorothy@blakemorezone.co.uk**, or visit my website at **sowaseed.uk** to explore more of my work and future books.

Thank you for reading, and for supporting gentle, faith-rooted fiction.

Don't miss out!

Visit the website below and you can sign up to receive emails whenever Dorothy Blakemore publishes a new book. There's no charge and no obligation.

https://books2read.com/r/B-A-GMGJF-VZCFJ

BOOKS 2 READ

Connecting independent readers to independent writers.

Also by Dorothy Blakemore

Brookleigh Bay
After the Wedding
The Potter's Heart
The Light Between Us

Watch for more at www.sowaseed.uk.

About the Author

Dorothy Blakemore is the author of the Brookleigh Bay series—faith-filled stories of love, healing, and second chances set in a close-knit coastal village.

A retired teaching psychologist, she brings emotional depth and gentle realism to her writing. She lives in Whitley Bay and publishes with Mustard Seed Press.

Read more at www.sowaseed.uk.

www.ingramcontent.com/pod-product-compliance
Lightning Source LLC
LaVergne TN
LVHW051015080826
845145LV00009B/2631

* 9 7 8 1 0 6 7 6 3 4 9 7 1 *